Janet Ambrose

The Ghost at Birkbeck Station

and

Other Terse Verse

To Ellie

Best wishes

Janet Ambrose

AUSTIN MACAULEY
PUBLISHERS LTD.

Copyright © Janet Ambrose (2017)

The right of Janet Ambrose to be identified as author of this work has been asserted by her in accordance with section 77 and 78 of the Copyright, Designs and Patents Act 1988.

All rights reserved. No part of this publication may be reproduced, stored in a retrieval system, or transmitted in any form or by any means, electronic, mechanical, photocopying, recording, or otherwise, without the prior permission of the publishers.

Any person who commits any unauthorized act in relation to this publication may be liable to criminal prosecution and civil claims for damages.

A CIP catalogue record for this title is available from the British Library.

ISBN 9781786930514 (Paperback)
ISBN 9781786930521 (Hardback)
ISBN 9781786930538 (E-Book)
www.austinmacauley.com

First Published (2017)
Austin Macauley Publishers Ltd.
25 Canada Square
Canary Wharf
London
E14 5LQ

About the Author

Janet Ambrose was born in 1937 and had a varied career as secretary, judo teacher, physiotherapist and local government officer for Lewisham Council, the GLC and finally getting her grey hairs in Lambeth's Housing Development Department.

After early retirement she pursued her hobby of mandolin-playing and attended Goldsmith's College, London, where she gained a B.Mus. in 1996.

Throughout her life she has been involved in local politics and community work having joined the Labour Party around 1960 and West Beckenham Residents' Association around 1970 where she served as Planning Officer, Chairman and finally was appointed as President in 2012.

She is an enthusiastic dog-owner, member of the Holiday Fellowship, Greenpeace, the Field Studies Council and the Woodland Trust. She is a keen conservationist and was a leading campaigner for the conversion of South Norwood Sewage Farm into what now is South Norwood Country Park in the borough of Croydon.

After a lifetime of living in Beckenham she moved to Addiscombe, Croydon in 2011.

Contents

Foreword

A wise old lady once gave me a beautifully– printed motto:-

Give me a sense of humour Lord
The grace to see a joke
To get some happiness in life
And pass it on to other folk.

This may have been my inspiration for recording those hilarious happenings which would otherwise have been forgotten, the irritations turned around into laughter, and other elements of stupidity which reflect endearing aspects of human behaviour.

I hope the scatological references are not offensive, but people do find these funny. Likewise, may I be forgiven for political poems with which some readers may disagree. If so, do skip them – but they reflect my feelings at the time of writing.

Criticisms in verse sometimes hit home more effectively than direct comment. Perhaps one of my more rewarding moments was when someone overheard impervious members in Bromley Council's corridors of power saying, "Oh dear. They're writing poetry about us now."

I don't think I changed much in this respect, but I hope the reader can enjoy my efforts, and that we can laugh with each other.

Janet Ambrose, January 2012

The Ghost at Birkbeck Station

Birkbeck Station's quiet and sleepy,
But after dark it gets quite creepy.
Remote from passing friendly faces
And local pub "W.G.Grace's",
It's bordered on the Southern side
By Beckenham Cemetery – long and wide.
With platform each for tram and train
It's just a branch line – nothing main.

One dismal autumn eve while waiting
For a tram, contemplating
A night at Croydon's Fairfield Halls
(With ticket booked for middle stalls),
I happ'd to take a casual glance
O'er the graves. Then like a trance
I saw a phantom standing there
Floating six feet in the air.
A transparent woman – silent – still,
In coat and dress – no wisp or frill.

Down my spine there shot a shiver;
Through my hair I felt a quiver.
I closed my eyes and looked away,
But still she's there as clear as day.
So just don't look! I'll turn my back!
I'll face the British Railway track …
Where the same woman – now solid and plain
Was standing, waiting for a train.

Oh what relief! So now undaunted
I sought the reason I was haunted.
It didn't take too much detection
To find my ghost was a reflection
On the tramstop shelter rear.
This had caused my spurt of fear,
And this trick of light the explanation
Which laid the ghost ... at Birkbeck Station.

In memory – *a childhood tear*

Alas poor Doris–
I loved her a lot
But she was a chicken...
And went in the pot.

A True Story

I was shopping in Sainsbury's at Croydon.
T'was getting near red nose day,
When I saw a pile of red noses
On a very large central display.

Then somebody knocked the lot flying.
Red noses shot everywhere.
And then no-one was crying
But laughter was filling the air.

The laughter came from the noses
And as they rolled over the floor
People kicked them about accidentally,
Which made them laugh even more.

No-one else seemed to think it was funny
As each nose by their feet had a poke.
They were too busy spending their money
To have time to enjoy a good joke.

Now I am by nature quite thrifty.
My money's not wasted or blown.
And yet I forked out three pounds fifty
For a laughing red nose of my own.

Now if ever I feel a bit dismal
(And we all have these spells I suppose)
I can conquer these moods quite abysmal
By tapping my lovely red nose.

And as I join in with its laughter
And feel my spirits uplift
It reminds me of that day in Sainsbury's
When their central display went adrift.

The Egg

A Dowager, full of pomp and state
Came walking down to breakfast ... late.
Said "Waiter I'd like something light
"To satisfy my appetite.
"I don't want marmalade or toast,
"So what d'you think would suit me most?"

He said "We've choices wide among
"Which there's some lovely tongue."

Her screams were heard from North to South
"Eat something FROM AN ANIMAL'S MOUTH?
"Ugh. Whatever next, I beg?
"Now, hurry, man – BRING ME AN EGG!"

(In case the penny hasn't dropped
Although the poetry has stopped –
A chicken's end has a concealed junction
So it can carry out a dual function.
And if food from an animal's mouth doth come
Is it worse than food from an animal's… oooops!)

A passing thought or two

I wonder, can anyone here explain
Why we joyously wave at a passing steam train.
When walking we waved as one thundered by
And the passengers smiled and waved back in reply.
Yet the same folk would probably just glare at us
If we waved as they passed on a red London bus.

The short person's lament

Mirror, mirror on the wall
Why do you think I'm six feet tall?
It would make me so much gladder
To be provided with a ladder.
Then I'd see my face instead
Of just the top bit of my head.

A pain in the back

Why do so many chairs slope back?
Is it simply so they can easily stack?
Don't the makers have the wit
To realise chairs should help you sit
In a way that can relax
The tired muscles of our backs?
Don't they realise that it's grim
To feel the pressure of the rim
Behind the thighs so that the knees
Are stretched and you can't sit at ease?
They're only any use at all
For a jack-knifed posture if you're six feet tall.

Ode to a critic
(who criticised my verse)

You remind me of my dear old aunt.
She needed a sense of humour transplant.
Her doctor said, "I must confess"
"It can't be done on NHS
"D'you think you could pay the fee
"To have the job done privately
"Or else have you got the endurance
To look for some cheap health insurance?"
But dear old auntie, full of guile
Said, "Oh blow[1] it, I'll just learn to smile!"

---

[1] *The raconteur may wish to substitute a stronger word which is outside the range of this transcript.*

Beware of Room 18

Hawkswood College at Stroud
(An old fashioned place you'll agree)
Has no en-suite rooms for the crowd
Just a communal W.C.… so

When you're put in a room which is next to the loo
You hear everyone's tinkle and everyone's poo.

As you try to sleep you lie there and wonder
When persons unknown will wake you with their thunder.

Then on using the flush you hear waters roar…
And some of the buggers don't half slam the door.

So managers please have some mercy and pity
For the resident dumped in the room which is shitty

And ask yourselves, "Isn't some recompense due
"To the person dumped in the room by the loo?"

*…Well, their customer satisfaction questionnaire
did invite comments,
but alas there was no refund or response.*

…So why didn't you get married?

Well,
When I took up judo
Quite a few years ago,
I lost my poor lover
Through learning to throw.

"I bet you can't throw me,
"My darling," he said.
I thought I would try and…
He fell on his head

The moral for every
Potential first dan
Is "Keep doing judo"
"But never on your man"

Sweet Betsy and Mike

Do you remember Sweet Betsy from Pike?
She practised judo on her boyfriend, "Mike".
She tried Uchimata[2]
Now Mike is in pain.
He'll never practise with Betsy again!

Long Mike and Sweet Betsy attended a dance
Betsy was dreaming and while in her trance
She took poor Mike by his sleeve and lapel.
What happened then I expect you can tell.

The moral for them who wants love to run sweet
Is "Don't try to sweep your old man off his feet
"Don't try to throw him whatever you do
"But be ready to jump when he tries to throw you!"

---

[2] *"Uchimata" – the term for the inner thigh throw.*

... With apologies to Des

The queen potato, large and stern
Addressed her three princesses in turn
Saying "Have regard to affairs of state.
"Each find yourselves a suitable mate.

Full of laughter full of fun
Up jumped princess number one.
She said "Mama I'm not absurd
"I'll happily wed dear King Edward."

The queen said "Yes dear. He will do,"
Then quickly turned to princess two,
Who said "My romance you won't spoil
"As I'm in love with Jersey Royal"

Her Ma responded, "I Agree."
And then glared down at number three
Who said, with somewhat nervous voice,
"Oh dear, Des Lynam is my choice."

"Yeeeou can't wed him," screamed her mater
"Ugh, he's only a common tater"!

Motorway Madness

A driver on a motorway
(I think it was some time back last May)
Abruptly shuddered to a halt
And said "Oh I'm a stupid dolt
"I packed my bag and went to the bank
"But I clean forgot to fill my tank
"And now I'm stuck and I'll be late."
Then he heard a voice say
"What's up Mate?"

He looked to the left and he looked to the right
But there wasn't a solitary soul in sight.
Then on his car bonnet he saw a bee.
He said "Was that you spoke to me?"
The bee said "Yes, No need to shout
"There's certainly no-one else about.
"I know, you've had a night on the town
"And you've run out of gas and you've broken down.
"Well, I think I can help. Can you hang on a mo?"
The chap said, "You're joking. I'm stuck. I can't go."

So he waited, and after a minute or two
A whole swarm of bees came into view.
One said "Take the cap off." and with no more ado
Into his petrol tank every one of them flew.
Then they all went quiet as though concentrating.
Then out of the tank, in a cloud emanating,
They victory rolled and quickly dispersed,
Apart from the one who'd spoke to him first.

He said "Start her up then. No time to delay."
The car roared into life, and as he drove away
The chap said, "What's in there? What's happened to me?"
The insect replied, "Ain't you heard of BEE PEE?"

The trip in Suffield Road

(courtesy of Stewart Fleming School and
Bromley Council)

When fitting an inspection hatch
For school TV they left a patch
Of footway which was undulating.
A nasty hazard thus creating.

To remedy this bumpy ground
They slapped some pink cement around
The hatch, but still a bit was high
On which I stumbled by and by.

So after nearly falling hard
I sent the Council a green card
And in due course had a reply
With a job number – rather high.

Two hundred and six thousand, six hundred and fifty-four
With letter saying 'ring us if you want to know more'.
So six months later again I tried
And this time the Inspector for the roads replied.

He looked at the mound and scratched his head,
And after a little thought he said,
"The footway slopes but the hatch is flat.
"You can't expect us to remedy that!"

"Though there's a hump and a bump and a lip,
"For insurance purposes, it's not a trip."
Implying "If you tumble, duck,
"I'm sorry but it's your hard luck."

27

On hearing this I looked about
For someone with a bit more clout,
And in due course a letter sent
To THE PORTFOLIO HOLDER FOR THE
ENVIRONMENT.

I really must give him his due,
'Cos he came and looked at it too
And said the problem would need some thought
Because it was an unusual sort.

Imagine then my great delight
When the area around it was painted white,
And soon after the footway was thus patterned
The hump, the lip and the bump were flattened.

So now when rushing for tram or train
I trust no-one will trip again
And strangely, you know, you can get quite fond
Of a politician who waves a magic wand.

Fowl Play at Birkbeck Bridge, Elmers End Road

(Local Government Elections 2006)

At Birkbeck rail bridge SE20
There is pigeon mess a-plenty.
Lib-Dems to their eternal shame
In May's elections made the claim
(To give themselves electoral boost)
That they had remedied this roost
And had the bridge made pigeon-proof.
Oh, what a porkie, what a spoof.
Appalling mess still meets the eye.
So every time when you pass by
Or get a hit from pigeon splat,
Shout, "Foul play, Liberal Democrat!"

Traffic Calming
a warning to fellow residents

Bickley residents beware
As Bromley Council doesn't care.
If traffic calming is a mess
Don't expect them to confess.
They put our protests on a file
And quickly went into denial
About the dangers they'd created,
Warning of which we'd clearly stated.

If you think I make a fuss
Please come along and visit us
In Marlow Road SE20,
Where we've had bumps and knocks a-plenty,
Stress and Anger, tyres burst
Because by Bromley we've been cursed.

Speeding traffic still zooms by.
When turning left you wonder why
You're in the oncoming traffic lane.
It's no good trying to explain
The kerb extensions steer you there.
But Bromley Council doesn't care.

NB: Bromley Council actually replied to this in rhyme.

On fortnightly refuse collections

Oh councillors would it make you happy
To smell a decomposing nappy
Two weeks after the baby filled it
Just 'cos your officials willed it
Should be collected fortnightly?
It isn't nice you must agree.

Now those who live in mansions grand
Set in lots of open land
Are never going to get infested
Like we who live where it's congested.
So why do you want to fill our houses
With bluebottles rats and flies and mouses?
And don't forget there's those disgraces
Who rubbish dump in public places.

Until these points are solved endeavour
To let weekly collections last for ever.

The Lady of the Dance
Lest we forget...

I danced in the May when I went to number ten
And I danced in the June when we had a budget then
And we cut back your services and cut the wealthy's tax
And you all had to dance with me upon your backs.

Chorus:
> Dance then whoever you may be.
> "I was the lady of the dance" said she
> "And I'll lead you on whoever you may be
> "And I'll lead you on in the dance" said she.

So you danced when you felt my cuts begin to bite
And you danced if you died in the middle of the night
And you danced if you couldn't find a hospital bed
And I was still the lady of the dance, she said.

Chorus

So I danced in the Falklands and I had a Victory
A thousand were killed but the glory came to me.
Then one year later in the next election
I was swept back to power so the dance went on.

Chorus

So you danced if your children were taken into care
And you danced if they couldn't be placed anywhere
You could dance if you were deaf; dance if you were blind!
You all knew the lady of the dance wouldn't mind!

Chorus

Land of Hope and Tory

Land of hope and glory
That's what it used to be
'Til you voted Tory
And landed yourselves with me.

Deeper yet and deeper
My cuts would ever get
But we who helped the wealthy
Would make them wealthier yet.
We who helped the wealthy
Would make them wealthier yet.

'PAT'[3] Dog Bruno

Bruno was a 'PAT' dog
Just an ordinary chap.
He didn't pull upon the lead
or smell, or bite, or yap.

Occasionally Bruno thought
T'would add to his allure
To roll his neck and shoulders in-
to substances impure.

Once in a while he'd bark a bit
If fox was on the prowl,
And if disturbed when fast asleep
He'd give a little growl.

Now whether he was musical
Was very hard to say.
At our mandolin club
He'd pass the time away
Sitting quietly on the floor
At his boss's feet,
Thinking about tea-time when
He'd hope to get a treat.

But what he thought of Beethoven
Or Bartok, Brahms or Bach,
We never knew 'cos on this
Bruno kept us in the dark.

---

[3] *Pets As Therapy – special pets brought in to help patients recuperate
(originally a 'get-well' poem for a friend)*

To those who'd ail
He'd wag his tail
Saying "Keep your chins up, dear,
"Let's hope the worst's behind you now
"Look forward to next year."

And if anyone was musical
He loved to hear them play
Saying "Try to keep yourself in tune,
"Best wishes, B. and J."

(i.e. Bruno and Janet)

Sad, Sad, Sad Foal Farm (the animal rescue centre at Biggin Hill)

When my dog died, oh how I grieved.
Just like anyone bereaved.
Then gradually I felt more calm
And went by car over to Foal Farm.

I'd had a dog from them before
And so I thought I knew the score.
But with no reception kind and warm
I was curtly told "Fill in that form."

She said, "There's photos, but no dogs to view
"And don't ring us, 'cos we'll ring you."
It was later a shock on the phone to be told
"You can't have a dog from us. You're too old!"
"You may well think this is a pity
"But this was decided by our committee"
Implying I couldn't have one of their dogs
Because they thought I might soon pop my clogs.

Foal Farm you care for animals – true,
But spare a kind thought for bereaved owners, too.
Your reasoning may have had some foundations
But please take a course in public relations.

[Subsequently Foal Farm apologised and the perpetrator is no longer employed there]

The Tiddler on the Roof

You may know when you turn left at London Bridge
Station,
There was a walkway, or elevation
To Guy's Hospital, crossing over St. Thomas Street,
Where I walked with dog "Bruno" by my feet.
We'd hardly got as far as the middle
When Bruno thought, "Ooh, I must do a tiddle."
Imagine my panic and dismay
To see this sunlit golden spray
Emanating from Bruno's flow
Towards <u>pedestrians,</u> down below.

I prayed no-one would look to the sky
And get a twinkle in the eye.
Then from my position aloof
I saw there was an extended roof
Which stretched out a bit toward the road
And on which Bruno's tiddle flowed.

The moral of this you may surmise
Is that all dogs can take you by surprise
However carefully they're taught –
Especially when they're taken short.

NB: Keeping verse updated is rather hard
They've now closed that walkway to build a Shard.

The Nose

What a wonderful thing is a nose.
You humans can hardly suppose
The stimulation and verve
We dogs get from this olfactory nerve.

You see in colour but smell in black and white.
With us it reverses; smell is stronger than sight.
I know where Rover's tiddled and it's absolute bliss
To have a good sniff at Mr. Fox's piss.

I can tell what Fido had for lunch and which girls are on
heat
And the whereabouts of every cat living in our street.
And there's even a special smelly hue
Which surprisingly is unique to you.

So be patient when I sniff at every tree,
'Cos it's the Sun, Mail, Telegraph, Standard, Mirror and
Times to me.

My dog gets me into trouble again

Some lads in the park were playing cricket
When my dog grabbed their ball and then fell on their
wicket.
Now had they appealed with the usual shout
Would the batsman, not in his ground, be out?

Perhaps this question, you might agree,
Should really be referred to the M.C.C.

The disgraceful dog-owner

We don't expect you to confess
When you don't clear up your dog's mess,
But surely even you'll agree
It's horrible for all to see.
You're filthy and you make us frown.
<u>YOU LET ALL GOOD DOG OWNERS DOWN</u>!
And please don't bag it up then drop it.
It's foul and dangerous, so stop it.
Don't commit this canine sin.
Take it home or find a bin!

To the litterbug

If you drop rubbish in parks and grounds
You could be fined a thousand pounds.
Likewise if dropped out in the road,
So take it home to your abode.

If you are caught you will feel bitter
So be a dear and bin your litter.

Of Mandolins

When you play the mandolin
It helps if you are rather thin
If alas you're getting stout
The bowl goes in, where you stick out...
...A problem which is less by far
When playing banjo or guitar.

When you play the mandolin
Your fingers hurt where strings cut in.
Each fingertip smooth since you were born
Becomes encrusted with a corn
Some call it "hard skin"
That's just semantic.
But when you're out walking with a fella in the pale
moonlight
Corns on your fingertips aren't very romantic.

At Christmas

"When I'm coming", Santa tells
"You won't hear my jingle bells"
Because he adds with jovial grin,
"I've taken up the mandolin
"And so my sleigh goes through the snow
"Accompanied by a tremolo
"And when I'm braking with a swish
"I finish with a lovely g
                          l
                           i
                            s
                             s
                              s
                               s
                                .
                                 .
                                  .

From the winter of 2010-2011

When I was a child
(That's before kids were 'cool')
We didn't let snow
Stop us going to school.

No boots then, just shoes.
I recall my feet froze.
I used to get chilblains
On some of my toes.

At our school one day
The headmistress said
School milk should be heated
We had cocoa instead.

She sent us home early
As the journey took longer
But as we struggled through
I think we grew stronger.

The children today
Make me feel really vexed
"No school 'cos there's snow
In the playground" – what next?

I expect very soon
They will start to complain
"We can't go to school
'Cos we think it might rain!"

A New Year Diminution...

At Christmas time one overeats –
     too many treats
of cake and pud –
     and one consumes more than one should.

So to January we come
     with bulging tum
and resolution to dispose
     of this subcutaneous adipose.

Now if like me you're born under Taurus
     (and I don't want to go on too long, or I'll bore us)
But you'll know it causes much distaste
     if absolutely anything goes to waste.

So first to finish the remains
     of all those foods which cause weight gains.
So I've used the cream, and ate the chocs
     (which came in boxes and in blocks).

I've ate the crisps, and the cheeses
     as ever outward my waistline eases.
Then just as my diet's about to begin
     another late present of chocs comes in.

I'll finish those then do my best –
     to diet. Now I'm in earnest.
It's serious now. I **will** begin.
     But dear oh me – what's in that tin?

I open it and before my eyes
there's half a dozen left-over mince pies!
I put them there and then forgot.
Now I've got to eat the lot!

My good intentions never vary, but now it's almost
February!

Doodlebugs

I well remember the chug-a chug-a chug-a-chug
Of an approaching doodlebug.
It sent us running helter-skelter
Down the garden to our shelter.
Where we crouched with hands clamped to our ears
Trying to suppress the fears
Of secret weapon up on high
Somewhere above us in the sky.

Then silence … as the noise cut out
Fifteen seconds – or there about.
Fifteen seconds with terror filled
Would it land on us. Would we be killed?
Then booohm! We ran out with relief
To see who may have come to grief
And watch with awe the huge black cloud
Expanding – like a funeral shroud.

Such was the panic thus created
That children were evacuated.
I recall the train that took us forth
To somewhere strange, away up North.
With my big sister, it was O.K.
But ahh the wonderful, wonderful day
When, ten months on, Mum came for us.
Oh lots of joy and lots of fuss.

On getting back I was nearly eight
And thought "There's no bombs: This is great"
For bombs had always been the norm
And daily life took the form
Of sirens, 'all clears', blackout at nights,
Of flashes and bangs and lots of bomb sites,
And sometimes being taken to task
If I went to school without my gas mask.

Now there's no more bombs, no more time in the shelter.
We can safely sleep – there's no more helter skelter.
There's no more leaving our warm beds at night,
No more spoilt meals, no more, "Put out that light."
Oh joy! No more bombs, and even today
It's some seventy years on and I still feel that way.

***

This is history and I hope it's not a bore,
But to appreciate peace, must you live through a war?

A Bomb in Beckenham
(an infant's perspective)

I was two or three
On my mother's knee
On a bus...
There was such a fuss...

A lady threw herself down to the floor
Into the bus's corridor.
Big sister cried "People are spinning around
"They fall on the pavement; they fall on the ground.
"And the glass in shop windows is all falling in..."
"What was it," I wondered, "that caused all this din?"

Mother was shouting (and her voice was a squeal)
"The driver, the driver held onto the wheel.
"He held the wheel. He held the wheel
"Please tell the driver how grateful I feel."
The conductor said, "Madam; we all do our best
"And holding the wheel is just one more test."

I was puzzled for many a year to come
About 'holding the wheel' as screamed out by my mum.
I understood 'wheels' on which buses ran,
And I knew that the driver up front was a man.
I was like a spectator with panic all round
And I'm sure he did not jump down to the ground
To hold one of the wheels, and why would he do it?
Oh, a steering wheel – some years later I knew it.

I was too young to understand what I was hearing
Or to know that a wheel in a bus was for steering
As I still sat there on my mother's knee
Unaware of the near catastrophe
Which could so easily have finished us
On that Beckenham 227 Bus.[4]

---

[4] *This was probably in 1940, and in Beckenham High Street. I never knew whether the people spinning around and falling were just knocked over by the blast or whether they were killed. They say that you don't hear the explosion of the bomb that kills you... I heard no bang on that day.*

A historical misunderstanding

Now Hitler was a nasty brute
So why was I doing a Nazi salute?
Photographed with hand held high
I can't imagine. Why oh why?

But then the thought occurred to me
Someone had said "Hands up for tea!"

I wondered then if the Nuremberg rally
Had someone off-stage taking a tally
Of lots of folk who just like me
Put their hands up 'cos they wanted a cup of tea.

(Next time you're in a group and someone says, "Hands up for tea!" ... just observe!)

Bees in my Bonnet and Post Ghost poems

Foreword

The Ghost at Birkbeck Station was my first really successful verse, and I have always been grateful to that lady (whoever she was) who scared the life out of me on that memorable evening, many years ago. I therefore decided to include her again in this (my second volume) as an introduction. Some readers may have missed her first time, while others may enjoy the spine tingling scare of this <u>true</u> story once again.

I have had great pleasure in putting this second collection together and hope this may be shared with you. Again, please forgive or skip the political references if you disagree with them, and remember – if you annoy me – you might go down in poetry.

Janet Ambrose
March 2016

Bees in my Bonnet

If something irritates me
I put it into verse.
I something irritates me
Nothing could be worse
Than letting it buzz around
All day inside my head,
And so to get it off my chest
I write it down instead.

I turn it into poetry
Just like this little sonnet
This is the way that I release
THE BEES INSIDE MY BONNET.

The Ghost at Birkbeck Station

Birkbeck Station's quiet and sleepy,
But after dark it gets quite creepy.
Remote from passing friendly faces
And local pub "W. G. Grace's",
It's bordered on the Southern side
By Beckenham Cemetery – long and wide.
With platform each for tram and train
It's just a branch line – nothing main.

One dismal autumn eve while waiting
For a tram, contemplating
A night at Croydon's Fairfield Halls
(With ticket booked for middle stalls),
I happ'd to take a casual glance
O'er the graves. Then like a trance
I saw a phantom standing there
Floating six feet in the air.
A transparent woman – silent – still,
In coat and dress – no wisp or frill.

Down my spine there shot a shiver;
Through my hair I felt a quiver.
I closed my eyes and looked away,
But still she's there as clear as day.
So just don't look! I'll turn my back!
I'll face the British Railway track…
Where the same woman – now solid and plain
Was standing, waiting for a train.

Oh what relief! So now undaunted
I sought the reason I was haunted.
It didn't take too much detection
To find my ghost was a reflection
On the tramstop shelter rear.
This had caused my spurt of fear,
And this trick of light the explanation
Which laid the ghost at Birkbeck Station.

V J Morning
(the end of World War 2)
15th August 1945

Grandma danced
Grandma pranced
Grandma who was so severe,
Grandma who we viewed with fear.
Lifting skirts, showing knees
This grandma could never please
Came out with this epitome,
"My son, my son is coming home,
"My son is coming home."

Months later at the railway station
Grandma, still full of elation
Approached a young man from the train.
Smiled, and started to explain
"I've come here to meet my son
"From Burma, now the war is won."

He looks at her through sunken eyes
He looks at her, and then replies

"…I am your son."[5]

---

[5] *Leading Aircraftman R. H. N. Ambrose*

Nelson Mandela

I once went up to Trafalgar Square
… And Nelson Mandela was there,
Though old and frail he made a plea
For the world to eradicate poverty.

Bob Geldof was there standing by
Keeping a worried watchful eye
On this lone figure who wanted to stay
To share time with the crowd on that cold cloudy day.

Persuaded to leave he was helped to his car.
It was wonderful seeing him, tho' from afar.
On the other side of Trafalgar Square…
Nelson Mandela was there.

Now alas he has gone,
But he will live on
As his gentle smile and forgiving grace
Has made our world a better place.

Beware the Stirrer
(for those who live in retirement flats)

When you are old and live alone
Sometimes you are inclined to moan
And get yourselves into a tizzy
Simply 'cos you are not busy

So to relieve this boring life
You like a little bit of strife.
Perhaps complaining gives some status
Or at least fills up a hiatus.

You take a pessimistic view
'Cos you do not have enough to do.
Supposed misdeeds you will refer
To your development manager...

Who hopefully won't take the bait
If sometimes you exaggerate.
She'll need diplomacy and tact
To sort out what is actual fact.

Sometimes she may find it wise
Simply to apologise.
Just calm the brow and let it rest
As this may be the course that's best.

We might get on each other's nerves
But some are simply mischievous ...
As when you're old and live alone
Sometimes you are inclined to moan.

On the Last Saturday in October

Early evening turned to night.
We've put the clocks back
It's not right.
I hate it and I bet you rue it.
Why oh why do we have to do it?

If perchance you agree,
Then drop a line to your M.P.
To ask that without hesitation
Please to initiate legislation.

'Cos we'll be healthier happier and stronger
If our light evenings lasted longer.
For fewer mishaps and less crime
Let's keep to British Summertime!

Writer's Block

"...   ?
          ...
                    ...
                    ..   ?
                         .
          .   ...
                              ..
                                   ....
                                        "

In writer's block
The brain doth lock.
It takes a rocket
To unlock it.

The Dandelion

Do not decry the dandelion.
Don't say that it's a weed.
'Cos as a medicinal herb
It's valuable indeed.

Do not decry the dandelion
Its beauty is untold
Closely cluttered petals
Bright yellow, even gold.

The honeybees adore them
And visit in the morn
But you must get up early
To see them after dawn.

Do not decry the dandelion
Its dark green leaves invite us
To add them to our salads
If suffering from cystitis.

Coffee is made from its roots
And won't keep you awake,
And the juice helps many ailments
If bitterness you can take:-

Silicic acid, sulphur,
Calcium. Manganese,
Potassium and vitamins
Will many an illness ease.

So don't decry the dandelion
It isn't "Just a weed".
It's the most precious of all plants –
A medicine chest indeed.

The Falklands Fiasco

Remember old Jim Callaghan?
Argentina threatened war
So he sent a submarine out to
Patrol the Falklands shore.

He did it very quietly
But made sure the Argies knew.
There was no Falklands war then
'Cos Jim was right on cue.

But when Galtieri tried again
Thatcher looked away.
She cancelled our patrol ship[6]
And let the whalers stay…

On Georgia where they'd trespassed –
Just testing out the ground,
Argentina then invaded –
Our Navy was not around.

And she became a heroine
Of a war, but if she'd tried
She could easily have stopped it.
So a thousand poor souls died.

It is a sorry fact of life
But one that we must master –
You get no credit or reward
For averting a disaster.

---

[6] *HMS Endurance*

Did Thatcher really want that war?
Her prospects then were grim.
It never would have happened if
She'd learned from dear old Jim.

This turned her fortunes right around.
She really did not mind
That someone took the blame for her –
Lord Carrington resigned!

Ten million pounds to bury her
That's what I heard them say.
It happened thirty years ago
And still we have to pay.

The Dilemma

My genes and chromosomes, family tree or stemma
Cannot resolve the socialists' dilemma
Of providing for those who can't help themselves and are
needy
Against those who do help themselves and are greedy.

This is regrettably the old old story
Told by those who do help themselves and are Tory.

...And They Say Northing Rhymes with "Orange"

When seeing a rainbow
The red doth impinge
On the next colour
A brilliant orange.
The spelling is different
But when spoken it rhymes
The problem is solved then
For now and all times.

The Undeaf

Pity the undeaf,
Both in bass and treble clef.
With vans reversing from afar
And radios booming from a car,
Understand the fears
Of bombardment of the ears.

Sumari warriors of Japan
Discovered sound waves could or can
Be a weapon of attack
With enemies suffering. Alack,
As a victim I know why.
Such assaults were called "Kei-ii".

Some people into microphones bellow.
Last week an otherwise kindly fellow
Became a weapon of assault
(Though it may not have been his fault)
I left his lecture feeling wild.
Suffering from concussion – mild.

You may think we make a fuss
As there are just a few of us.
As ambulance and police cars' wail
Upon our delicate ears assail.
We are not all Mutt and Geoff.
So PLEASE consider the undeaf.

Secret Weapon

I sat on the doorstop
Podding peas
And heard "Janet, come down to the shelter"
With my mum's colander
On my knees
And heard "Janet! – Come down to the shelter"

I said "Just a minute."
"I'm nearly through.
"I've only got two more
"To do."

Then for some reason
I don't know why
I chanced to look up
To the sky.

There was a sight I'll ne'er forget
A sinister silent silhouette…
A DOODLEBUG with noise cut out.
"I'm coming Mum. No need to shout…"

'Cos Janet ran down to the shelter.

(It must have landed in a nearby road
As I don't remember hearing that one explode.)

Christianity?
(Ode to church manager who complained in writing when their hall hirers were asked to reduce disco noise)

If the Church cannot accept a plea
To show a little sympathy
To the frail and elderly
Then what is Christianity?

It really does bring shame on you
As your Church lettings take the view
That booming bass and shouting too
Should wreck the lives of old folk who
Suffer by living next to you.

Boom Boom Boom Boom!
Sounds reverberate through each room
Thump Thump Thump Thump!
Relentless noise, and then your trump...

Just to make a greater strain
Your manager says we must refrain
From even going to complain
To those who cause this thumping pain.

You must know how this booming sound
Impacts upon the weak housebound
(and some can hardly move around)
As their TV volume is drowned.

So if the Church cannot accept a plea
To show a little sympathy
Towards the frail and elderly
Then what is Christianity?

6th August 2013

Dear Janet

Saturday Evening Hire

We write to enquire whether it was you and your dog that entered our Centre on Saturday to complain to our hirers. Please disregards this letter and accept our apologies if it was not. However, if it was then we write request that in the future you do not, under any circumstances, enter the building again for the purpose of interrupting a party.

Please be aware that the Centre hires out it facilities in accordance with a premises licence issued by the London Borough of Croydon. The licence authorises the carrying out of licensable activities; films, sporting events, live music, amplified recorded music, performances of dance, the provision of facilities for making music, dancing and the sale by retail of alcohol between the hours of 9:00 until 22:00 Sunday-Thursday and 9:00 until 23:00 Friday and Saturday.

The event on Saturday was a private family celebration and the Centre was not open to the general public and should not have been accessed by anyone other than invited guests. Our hirers have complained that someone from Court, entered the Centre uninvited, interrupted a private party to complain about the lights and music. Going forward, should you have a comment on how the Centre is used, please do

so directly to the Parish Office, Monday-Friday 9am-2pm,
we will then be able to help you where possible.

With Kind Regards

Centre Manager

When making Church hall bookings
Is it not the fashion
To temper profits
With a little compassion.

Keeping Young

Table tennis is a sport
That every senior citizen ought
To play or at least have a go
Despite reflexes being slow.

A little ball up in the air
You whack it, but it isn't where
You thought it was
But that's because
You went and took your eye off it
But do not blame yourself a bit
'cos it occurs to everyone
Now and then, but it's all fun.

There's elegant ladies seen to crawl
Under chairs to find the ball
Which quite often goes astray
During their exuberant play.

The exercise is really great
Improving your respiratory rate,
Muscle tone and suppleness,
So in the end you must confess:-

That if you take it up today
You'll get better as you play,
As table tennis is a sport to
Take up now. You really ought to.

The Coach
(Being one hired by HF Holidays Ltd
To take guests to National Trust
Properties at Dove Dale, Derbyshire)

They said it was state of the art
But it rattled and bumped from the start
The noise caused some moans
But my poor old bones
Were virtually shaken apart

Hadrian's Wall
(On Nora's HF Holiday: "Easy
Walking and Sightseeing")

Although the weather is fine
As I go up and down each incline,
I don't want to bore 'er
By complaining to Nora
But her idea of easy walking isn't mine.

Goodbye Waistline I Must Grieve You

I loved my jeans
They fitted well
Until my waist
Began to swell.

Now willpower is
The only means
To slim my waist
To fit my jeans.

Chance Encounters

"It's a different world," the lady said
"I'm caring for a dog called 'Fred'
"Now lots of people say 'Hello'
"And I get smiles where 'ere I go.

"Complete strangers passing by
"(Usually with averted eye)
"Now often greet me with a smile
"And like to stop and talk a while!

"I'm so happy now
"I think I ought-a
"Hang on to 'Fred' but
"He belongs to my daughter."

"Tilly's" Conscience

There's a dent in the duvet
I'm sure you will agree
That the dent in the duvet
Was <u>never</u> made by me.

The dent in the duvet
Is round and slightly warm
Yes, I suppose you could say
It does match my form.

In the dent in the duvet
Did you say there was some hair?
Well surely then it must be yours
It's not mine I declare.

Oh that dent in the duvet
She grumbled and she grumbled.
I hate to admit it but…
I think that I've been rumbled.

Salvation for the Planet

Could we trap the energy from a wagging tail
As it goes back and forth like a force ten gale?
Though some wag fast and some wag slow
All we need is a dynamo
And batteries to store the amps and ohms
To be used to heat our chilly homes.

Imagine the economy and joy
By merely saying "What a good boy."
We'd save our money and our planet.
Well, it's just an idea.

Yours truly

Janet

The Pet's Blessing Service

One cat, 30 dogs and a big fat snail.
All but one of them sporting a tail.
All were quiet, bar one, alack, alack
But he was discreetly moved to the back.

Each was blessed with a stroke and a pat
And afterwards I only hoped that
We didn't leave even a solitary flea
And the Vicar washed his hands before having his tea.

Bath Night

Bathing dogs you may agree
Is not a job done easily.
In trying to keep Fido in
It's you that gets soaked to the skin.
And then he shakes –
You dread that rhythm.
You're so wet now
You could get in there with 'im.

The smell from Hell

Her perfume really does repel.
She cannot have a sense of smell.
I fear this can cause altercation
As others gasp for ventilation.

Not just a scent but more a gas
Which lingers long alas, alas,
You always know when she's passed by.
Why does she use it, why oh why?

I wonder is the analysis
Olfactory paralysis
Resulting from a diagnosis
Of injury to the proboscis.

Be warned

Before setting out I ate a nut.
The tickle in my throat remains.
If you eat a nut before reading verse
You haven't got much in the way of brains.

Alice

I felt grateful to Alice
In her wheelchair
At West Croydon Tramstop
Just sitting there.

No hands; no legs.
Yet quite content
On this warm summer night which
In Croydon she'd spent.

She'd been playing bingo.
No luck I'm afraid,
But how I admired
The effort she'd made.

Getting out to enjoy life
While stuck in that chair,
With a mouthstick to guide it
She could go anywhere.

Then two girls who knew her
Paused for a chat;
Lit a cigarette for her.
She was pleased about that.

And when the tram came
She decided to stay
Just a bit longer to
While the evening away.

Then the girls in the tram
Said she lived all alone,
With carers to help her,
But they ne'er heard her moan.

They both really loved her.
She was never forlorn –
A body and a head –
That's how she was born.

And I thought about us
With our grumbles and grouses.
Sometimes too nervous
To leave our safe houses.

So I'm grateful to Alice
With my eyes opened wide,
And guessed she had suffered
From thalidomide.

We left her at West Croydon
Puffing away
Completely content
At the end of that day.

Yes, I'm grateful to Alice
Who showed without fuss
That life can go on
What 'ere fate throws at us.

The Baton

The conductor dropped his baton.
It clattered to the floor
Someone picked it up for him
But he did it once more.

Did he need glue upon his hand
To make that baton stick?
Or perhaps the problem could be solved
By a length of elastic.

It reminded me of a time when once
Our conductor in a rage
Went and let his baton slip
It flew across the stage...

To hit a banjo vellum
With an almighty plop
And everyone was laughing
So the music had to stop.

Dear old Arthur Davidson
Conducted with such verve – that
He broke his baton on his stand
But he had one in reserve.

I've dropped my baton many a time
And seen smiles on many faces,
But NEVER let your baton drop
In Olympic relay races.

A Web of Intrigue

When waiting for a tram one day
I thought a little trick I'd play
Upon a spider, so I threw
A seed into her web and drew
That spider who thought "yum, yum, yum,
"Here's something to fill my tum."

She felt it and then with a 'bing'
Ejected the unwholesome thing.

I tried again to play this trick.
She twiddled it with her legs then "flick"
She shot the solid seed away
Disgusted that it was not prey.

"How long," I thought, "Could I deceive her?"
But the tram came then so I had to leave her.

Storm in a Teapot

Jim Wise he was a signal lad.
A signal lad was he.
And while learning about signalling
He had to make the tea.

For Arthur, the chief signalman
And he was old and strict
And issued our young Jimmy with
A very strict edict:-

"When you empty our big teapot
"(Its enamel large and red)"
"Don't tip it out the window
"Take it to the drain instead."

Now the signal box was up on high
(Such boxes often are)
And Jim thought going down to the drain
Was just a step too far.

So with Arthur busy signalling
He very carefully shook
That big teapot out the window
Hoping Arthur wouldn't look.

'Twas before the days of teabags
So the teapot took some shaking
To dislodge the loose tealeaves
Prior to the next tea making.

Now on a balmy summer day
All staff were tense and scared.
There'd been a nasty accident
Frayed nerves had not repaired.

The Brighton Belle approached the box
Oh what a lovely sight
As it zoomed along the railway track
In the bright sunlight.

But suddenly it was braking
And shuddered to a halt
With sparks a-flying from the wheels
And one enormous jolt.

Crockery was broken
Luggage tumbled from the racks
And the guard approached the signalbox
Along the railway tracks.

He's spoken to the driver who
Was furious indeed
And shouted to old Arthur
"My driver won't proceed…

"Till he know why you waved at him
An emergency red flag."
"Oh Arthur" muttered Jimmy
And his jaw began to sag.

For standing by the window
Gripped firmly by his side
Was the RED ENAMEL TEAPOT
(which was very hard to hide.)

When they had a big enquiry
At the local main line station
Jim prayed they'd think the red flag was
Driver imagination.

He went on to be a signalman.
I know he wasn't fired,
'Cos he told me this true story
Ten years after he retired.

Feet on the Seat

When wearing trousers or a skirt
I hate having to sit in dirt.
The stuff that gets wiped from your feet
When resting your shoes on the seat.

I do not wish to sound a bore
But please keep your feet on the floor.

Caution

Before reading on
Dear reader you may feel
That my final poem
Is not for the genteel.
The story is true,
But do not rue.
Just tarry a while,
Although it might make you smile.

Railway Lines

My father was a railwayman
A railwayman was he,
And like many honest workmen
They had their own repartee.

The train to Littlehampton
Was named 'The Little Dick'
(I never understood this
'cos I'm innocent and thick)

And a train called 'The Old Lady'
Was the one that went to Ore.
I never understood this
'cos I'm something of a bore.

Now on a foggy winter night
The trains were in a mess.
(It happens on the railways
Now and then they must confess.)

So to save the people waiting
A brief message was sent
Using their own private lingo
But t'was done with good intent.

So at Streatham common station
A young porter newly trained
Used the public address system
But no one had explained

That he should amend the wording
So imagine all the fuss
When through the railway speakers
The message came out thus:-

He said "Passengers for the Little Dick
(while smiling though his teeth)
Please get on the Old Lady
And change trains at Haywards Heath."

Imagine the confusion
(Not just the fog was thick)
With passengers asking wildly
Where on earth's the Little Dick?"